# THE DARE

AN EROTIC ADVENTURE

VICTORIA RUSH

# VOLUME 22

JADE'S EROTIC ADVENTURES - BOOK 22

# COPYRIGHT

## ALSO BY VICTORIA RUSH:

THE
*Dinner*
PARTY
AN EROTIC ADVENTURE
VICTORIA RUSH

*Everybody's an exhibitionist in disguise...*

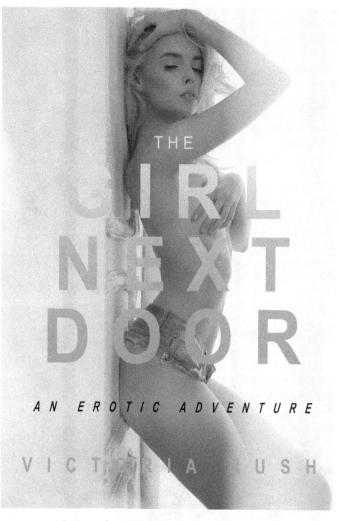

# THE GIRL NEXT DOOR

## AN EROTIC ADVENTURE

VICTORIA RUSH

*Spying on the neighbors just got a lot more interesting...*

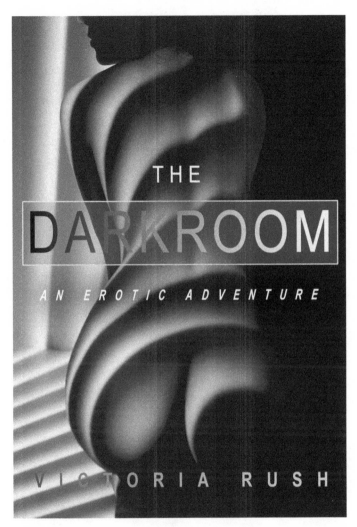

# THE
# DARKROOM
## AN EROTIC ADVENTURE

### VICTORIA RUSH

*Everything's sexier in the dark...*

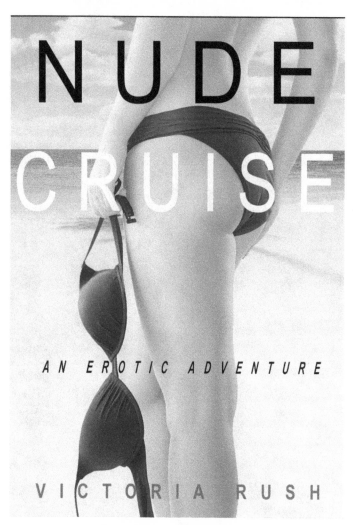

# NUDE

# CRUISE

## AN EROTIC ADVENTURE

### VICTORIA RUSH

*Some people get wet on a cruise for different reasons...*

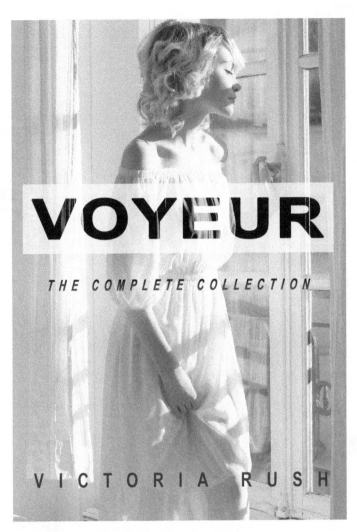

# VOYEUR

## THE COMPLETE COLLECTION

### VICTORIA RUSH

*Sometimes it's more fun to watch...*

*For the uninhibited...*

"**D**o you have any more cases that need my help?" I asked my best friend and certified sex therapist, Hannah, at our weekly get-together lunch.

Ever since the last time she'd invited me to sit in on one of her sessions, I'd fantasized about watching another one of her clients release her inhibitions while learning how to orgasm for the first time.

"I'm afraid Haley was a one-off," Hannah said. "That was definitely pushing the envelope in terms of how far I can take the concept of a guided session."

"But you said many of your clients are open to the idea of using a surrogate to help them overcome their fear of intimacy?"

"Yes, but bringing a third party into the equation is stretching the limits of client confidentiality."

"Not if they agree to it up front and sign a consent form."

"True. But I'm already drifting into unchartered territory using this unconventional form of sex therapy. I'm supposed to just *talk* to them, not watch them while they touch themselves."

I shook my head as I sliced into my grilled salmon.

"You just want to have them all to *yourself*," I winked.

"Maybe," Hannah smiled, noisily sipping her margarita. "But my hands-on approach seems to be working."

"How's Haley doing these days, anyway?" I said, wondering about the pretty co-ed I'd shared an intimate encounter with. "Is she still receiving treatment?"

"The last I heard, she was in a committed relationship with another girl at college. She said her sex life was very satisfying. Apparently, that blended session with you helped her turn the corner."

"Glad I could help," I said, crossing my knees under the table to quiet my tingling clit as I remembered watching Haley come between my legs. "Happy to hear we cured another dysfunctional patient."

"You shouldn't be so dismissive of other women's problems," Hannah said, looking at me disapprovingly. "The inability to orgasm is far more prevalent than people think, especially among women. It's often caused by a traumatic episode in their past or severe childhood repression. Not everyone's as lucky as you and me to have had a healthy upbringing."

"I'm sorry," I said. "You're right. I remember how unsatisfying my first marriage was. We were both raised in a conservative household that frowned upon any form of sexual expression before marriage. All Jason seemed interested in was doing the missionary position in the dark. I hardly even had a chance to get aroused before he popped off. It wasn't until I discovered sex with other *women* that I really learned to enjoy myself."

"You're lucky that you found a successful outlet for your desires at a relatively young age," Hannah nodded. "You've come a long way since then."

"Literally and figuratively," I chuckled. "I can hardly believe how enjoyable my sex life has become. My orgasms are stronger and more powerful than I ever imagined. And the best part is how *long* I can make it last. It's almost like I can turn it on and off at will, holding out until the best optimal moment."

"You mean coming simultaneously with your partner?"

"Most of the time, yes. But sometimes I like to wait until *she's* finished coming so I can concentrate on maximizing her pleasure."

"Maybe you should become a partner in my therapy practice," Hannah said, lifting an eyebrow. "It sounds like you've mastered your art. I could use another colleague to juggle my growing caseload."

"Ha!" I chuckled. "I'm afraid I could never have your discipline. I'd want to jump the clients every time instead of just talking them through their process of self-discovery. You'd lose your license in no time if you brought me on as a full partner."

Hannah paused for a moment as she took another sip of her cocktail.

"Maybe we should *test* the premise and see just how disciplined you really are. You say you can turn your desire on and off at will. I bet you wouldn't be able to control yourself so easily under the right circumstances."

"How do you mean?" I said, suddenly intrigued. "Under what circumstances?"

Hannah peered at me with a devilish grin.

"I think if we put you in a highly charged sexual situation and took away your ability to control the level of stimulation you received, that I could make you pop off whenever I wanted."

"Like *what*?" I said, leaning forward on the table. "What did you have in mind?"

"I've actually been thinking about this for a while," Hannah smiled. "Ever since we were at this same restaurant and you tried out my new sex toy under the table. It gave me some fresh ideas for how we could take it to the next level."

"That was pretty fucking hot," I nodded, feeling my panties begin to dampen at the thought of Hannah watching me squirm in my seat while I was surrounded by restaurant patrons quietly eating their meals. "How could you possibly make that any more arousing?"

"You have *no* idea," Hannah smirked, lifting her glass back up to her lips.

"Y ou can't leave me hanging like that!" I huffed, slamming my fists down on the table. "What kind of evil plan are you cooking up?"

Hannah peered at me as she took another bite of her shrimp salad. She was enjoying torturing me while my mind raced trying to imagine what she was concocting. When she swallowed her mouthful and washed it down with another sip of wine, I looked at her pleadingly, holding up my hands up in despair.

"What if we made your next sexual encounter a *one-way* affair, instead of a partnered experience?" she said.

"I've already tried every type of self-stimulation, using every toy imaginable. I think I've mastered the art of orgasm control via masturbation many times."

"Not when somebody *else* is controlling the toy."

My eyes suddenly flew open as I began to realize what Hannah had in mind.

"You mean using some kind of remote-control device?" I said. "I've heard about those and always wanted to give it a try."

"But not in a public place," Hannah smiled.

"*What!*" I said, jerking back in my chair. "Why would you want to do that? Wouldn't you already have all the power you need controlling the level of stimulation I receive watching me one-on-one?"

"That would be too simple," she said. "Kind of like a staring contest. In the absence of any distractions, it would just be mind over matter. But in a public setting it won't be so easy for you to stay focused. Plus, the consequences will be more serious if you do lose control."

I leaned forward and calmly ate another bite of my salmon, pretending to be unfazed.

"In the unlikely event that you could actually force me to reach orgasm on your terms, I'd just bite my lip and cross my legs, and no one would be any the wiser."

Hannah speared another piece of shrimp and raised it to her mouth, sucking on it teasingly.

"You're forgetting about that *other* feature of your sexual powers, which is your tendency to squirt when you come. If I can make you come in a public place, it will be almost impossible for everyone to not know what's happening."

I placed my hands on the edge of the table and pushed my chair backwards, scrunching my face in dismay.

"You are truly evil," I said. "What kind of sick person would dream up such a crazy scenario?"

"Your best friend and lover, for one," Hannah smiled.

"*You're on!*" I said, slamming my cocktail down on the table. "But what's in it for me if I win? Do I get a silent stake in your practice?"

"I think it's best we continue your role as a special consultant. I think we can use you more effectively as a mutual participant when the need arises. I was thinking of something we can *both* enjoy."

"Such as?"

"We've both talked about you much we'd love to go to Bora Bora. If I can make you lose control in public, you'll have to pay for the airfare. But if you're as good as you say you are, then *I'll* pay for the flights. What do you say–are you up for the challenge?"

"Possibly," I said, getting wetter by the moment imagining Hannah's crazy idea. "But exactly what kind of public settings are we talking about? It's only fair that you let me know what I'm getting myself into before I take the leap."

"No dice," Hannah said, crossing her arms. "If you're as skilled as you're making yourself out to be, it shouldn't matter what the setting is. Half the fun will be in your not knowing until we get there."

I paused for a long moment, running my eyes over Hannah's face, trying to divine her thoughts.

"Fine," I said, holding out my hand across the table. "But this'll be quite a switch for you–encouraging a client *not* to reach orgasm for a change."

"Quite the contrary," Hannah smiled, clasping my hand. "It's fully aligned with the vision of my practice. I've never yet had a client who failed to achieve sexual fulfillment. But as I always like to tell them–most of the fun is in the process of *getting* there."

"Okay, so now that I'm committed, tell me where you had in mind for this little experiment."

"Actually," Hannah said, "I have a *series* of places in mind, each one more challenging than the one before."

"But I thought you said this was a one-off proposition?"

"I said nothing of the sort. I only said that if you won, I'd pay for the flights to Bora Bora. If you want me to cover the cost of hotels, food, and all the other incidentals, you'll have to pass progressively tougher tests. We don't want to make this *too* easy for you, do we?"

I crossed my arms and huffed, putting on my best pouty face.

"It hardly seems fair," I said. "But I'm still game. Besides, either one of us can pull out at any time to lock in our gains, right?"

"I suppose so," Hannah shrugged. "But what would be the fun in that? Something tells me once you've tried the first experiment, you won't want to stop. I think you're going to find this whole thing quite titillating and exciting. This will be the most fun either one of us has had in a long time."

I pushed the rest of my half-eaten salmon dish to the side, suddenly no longer interested in eating.

"Okay, lay it on me then. Where are you planning to take me for the first test?

Hannah gulped down the rest of her margarita then peered at me with a lopsided grin.

"Church. More specifically, a *Catholic* church. You haven't been in quite a while, have you? This will be your chance to repent and atone for all your sins."

"It's not like I've broken any commandments or anything–"

"The Catholic Church still considers sex outside of marriage a mortal sin. So technically, you've been doing a ton of sinning since your marriage ended."

"Well I haven't been a practicing Catholic for ages," I snorted. "So my conscience is clear. This'll be a cakewalk. All I have to do is sit quietly in my pew, right?"

"Yes, but it'll be a *front-row* pew, in full view of the priest who'll be delivering the sermon."

"Okay, but I'll be fully clothed, right? It's not like there'll be anything for him to see..."

"Not if you can keep your composure and don't cum all over the floor," Hannah said, cocking her head playfully.

"I don't think I'll have any difficulty keeping my dick in my pants, in a manner of speaking. But you raise a good point. You can't expect me not to get a little wet while you're stimulating me. What will I be allowed to wear?"

"I assume you'll dress appropriately, wearing your Sunday best. A mid-length skirt and button-up blouse should do the trick. You should be able to hide a few dribbles that way, right?"

"I suppose so, but how will we muffle the sound of the vibrator buzzing inside my panties? There's likely to be other people sitting around me in adjacent pews..."

"Never fear," Hannah smiled, reaching into her purse and pulling out a U-shaped silicone sex toy. "I've been talking with our friend at the local Babeland store. She's given me the latest prototype of the We-Vibe vibrator to test." She held up a smaller device with two control buttons and a flywheel. "Complete with a Bluetooth remote control. And the best thing is that it's whisper-quiet.

"Here," she said, handing me the flexible device. "See for yourself."

She tapped one of the buttons on the remote and the thick side of the contraption began buzzing softly in my hand.

"Okay," I nodded, looking around me to see if any other restaurant patrons were distracted by the gentle hum of the object. "It's *quiet* enough, but which end goes inside?"

"The bulbous end is a natural G-spot stimulator. You place the flatter end against your clit, then pull the thing up tight against your vulva to keep it snugly in place."

I suddenly became mindful of the wetness permeating my panties as I imagined the device vibrating inside me, surrounded by a bunch of oblivious bystanders.

"Can I give it a try here, like we did last time?" I grinned.

"No way," Hannah said, pulling the toy out of my hands. "There'll be no trial runs for this or any future tests. You'll just have to wait until we get to the church."

"And where will *you* be sitting while this is all going down?" I said.

"Right next to you, of course. I'll want a front-row seat to watch all the action."

On Sunday morning, Hannah picked me up and drove me the two miles to our local church. The entire time I squirmed in my seat trying to imagine what it would be like having a vibrator buzzing inside me in the quiet chapel. When we got to the church parking lot, she pulled into a sheltered space then plucked the blue vibrator out of her purse and handed it to me, resting her arm on the seat cushion expectantly.

"*What?*" I said. "You don't trust me to put it in privately?"

"Not really," she smirked. "For all I know, you might pull on some adult diapers under your skirt to hide any unintended releases. Here," she said, handing me a plastic vial. "I brought some lube to make it go in easier."

"I don't need any," I said, pulling the vibrator out of her hands and placing it under my skirt. "I'm already plenty worked up thinking about this scenario."

"I hope you're wearing panties under that skirt," Hannah said, watching me shift my weight as I placed the device against my vulva. "We wouldn't want it popping out at an inopportune moment."

"I'll just have to leave that up to your imagination," I sneered, lifting my skirt halfway up my thigh. "Unless you need to inspect the goods to make sure I'm not cheating."

"I trust you," Hannah smiled, opening her car door. "Something tells me you're looking forward to this just as much as I am."

As we approached the entrance to the church, I noticed a familiar figure standing at the top of the steps greeting the incoming parishioners, and he made eye contact with me when Hannah and I approached the landing.

"Jade!" Father Fife said, holding out his hands to me. "I

haven't seen you in such a long time. It's so good to have you join us again."

"I'm sorry, Father," I said, placing my sweaty hand between his. "I've been a little distracted lately..."

"Life has a habit of getting in the way of the important things," he said. "We're just glad to have you whenever you can find time." He turned to Hannah, raising his eyebrows in curiosity. "And who's this lovely lady you've brought with you to attend our service today?"

"This is Hannah," I said, motioning toward my friend. "I thought I'd bring her along for moral support."

"Happy to have you, Hannah," Father Fife said, clasping Hannah's hands warmly. "The Lord knows we all need moral support wherever we can find it."

Hannah nodded politely, then the two of us walked through the entrance doors where I dipped my hand into the bowl of holy water and crossed my chest before continuing on toward the front of the chapel.

"*Jesus*," Hannah whispered, peering around the imposing shrine. "Is it just me, or did that feel a little creepy? All that talk about *having* us and that prolonged hand-holding. Hasn't he been paying any attention to the me-too movement?"

"I'm not sure any of that applies to men of the *cloth*," I chuckled. "But you better be careful about using the Lord's name like that around here. If anybody overhears you, you're liable to be burned at the stake."

The two of us stepped lively down the main aisle and finding a free spot in the front row, we took our seats flanked by two elderly couples. It was hard to imagine how Hannah would be able to use the remote-control device sandwiched so closely between other parishioners, and I crossed my legs, thankful for the brief respite. When everyone had filed into the chapel and the bell signaled the start of the service, a hush fell over the chamber and we all stood up as Father Fife walked onto the pulpit in his flowing robes.

"In the name of the Father, and of the Son, and of the Holy Spirit," he intoned solemnly.

"Amen," the congregation murmured in unison.

"The Lord be with you," he said.

"And with your spirit," the couples beside me retorted.

*What the hell have I gotten myself into?* I thought, feeling the flexible vibrator pressing against the inside of my closed legs. I didn't consider myself a terribly religious person, but being in this holy place surrounded by all the familiar rituals brought back all the old memories from my parents about the consequences of sinful behavior. *Surely getting secretly stimulated by a sex toy in the house of God will send me straight to hell.*

This was the point in the church service where everybody was supposed to take a moment to make a penitential act. While I listened to the other parishioners around me making their supplications, my knees began shaking as I made my own silent prayer for forgiveness.

"May Almighty God have mercy on us all," the priest said. "Forgive us our sins, and bring us to everlasting life."

"Amen," I joined in the congregation's response.

"Let us pray," Father Fife said, bowing his head.

As we closed our eyes and he began his opening prayer, Hannah nudged me with her knee and my mind raced with images of the pastor scornfully looking down at us while we played our blasphemous game. I peered up as he flapped his Bible closed, and caught him glancing in my direction.

"Through our Lord Jesus Christ, your Son," he said. "Who lives and reigns with you in the unity of the Holy Spirit, one God forever and ever."

"Amen," I said aloud, hoping he'd see me behaving like a good Catholic girl and turn his attention elsewhere.

He motioned for everyone to sit down and I was glad to get off my shaky feet onto the relative safety of the wooden pew.

"Good morning, ladies and gentlemen," he began his homily. "Today, I would like to talk with you about *morality*. Specifically, about the decaying state of society's morals in today's world. All around us we are surrounded by prurient symbols of modern decadence. First it was in the form of the printed word, then motion pictures, then the ubiquitous internet. It seems everywhere we turn, we are bombarded with profane and sacrilegious images."

I felt my heart pounding in my chest, like he was singling me out personally for my not-so-infrequent porn surfing.

"We seem to have forgotten," he railed, "the Lord's commandment that we shall not covet thy neighbor's wife. This admonition can be taken in its broadest context. Not only have many of you forsaken the sacred institution of marriage, but the egregious and widespread popularity of obscene *pornography* belies our unbridled lust and depravity. God slew Onan for spilling his seed, and so He will strike all others who practice self-abuse."

Hannah nudged her knee against mine, suddenly reminding me why we were here. I was glad that she hadn't yet had the opportunity to take out her remote-control device, and I prayed that we'd be able to get through most of the service without her rudely interrupting it. I'd already begun to regret agreeing to this little venture, and I hoped that somehow we'd be able to bypass this first phase in her experiment.

"I'd like you to pick up your Bibles," Father Fife said,

interrupting my thoughts. "And turn to Mark, Chapter 7, Verse 20."

Hannah and I reached down to pick up the bibles lying on the seat beside each of us, and we flipped to the indicated section.

"Read this passage with me, my friends," Father Fife instructed. "What comes *out* of a person is what defiles him," he enunciated, while the congregation quietly murmured along.

As I began to recite the passage along with him, I saw Hannah reach into her side pocket and place her closed hand between the book binding.

"For from within come evil thoughts," I continued reading as I peered out of the corner of my eye to see what she was up to.

"Sexual immorality, adultery, coveting, wickedness..." we read in unison.

Suddenly, I felt the interior end of the vibrator begin to tremble inside me and I stuttered, trying to finish the passage.

"Deceit...sensuality...envy..." I stammered, trying to catch my breath as I followed along. Hearing my labored recital, Hannah turned her head in my direction, acknowledging my silent suffering. She knew exactly what I was feeling and how difficult it was for me to remain composed as I read the script.

"All these evil things...come from *within*," I gulped as I began to feel the pleasure spread across my pelvic region. "And they defile a person."

"Consider these words carefully," the priest said, surveying my hunched-over posture. "For the Lord does not abide salacious thoughts and behavior. If you want passage into His Kingdom, you must be as pure and righteous as He."

He paused for a moment to let the message sink in, then he motioned with his two hands for us to be seated. I was grateful for the rest, and I froze upright in my chair trying to ignore the movement of the possessed instrument inside me.

"Let us consider for a moment *another* one of God's ten commandments," Father Fife continued. "Thou shall not commit *adultery*. The Lord made Eve from the flesh of Adam, and in so doing signified that forever more man shall be united to his wife as one..."

As Father Fife ramped up the intensity of his gayphobic critique, so did Hannah, furtively adjusting the flywheel on the remote-control device nestled under her palm in her lap. As she slowly increased the speed of the vibrations emanating inside my pussy, I squirmed on the bench, trying to restrain my rising passion.

"By rejecting the sanctity of marriage," Father Fife continued, glancing distractedly in my direction, "you have all *sinned*. In the book of Deuteronomy, we saw that God ordered adulterers be stoned to death. For your indiscriminate behavior, so shall the Lord indiscriminately smite thee."

*Jesus*, I thought. If that's what awaits a sinner for cheating on their spouse, I wonder what happens to someone who self-abuses herself while sitting for Sunday Service in a house of God. *Surely I'll burn in hell for this act of sacrilege.*

Just when I thought I was beginning to get control over the delicious sensations stimulating my insides, Father Fife instructed us to stand once again and recite another passage from the Bible.

"Please stand now and read Peter 1:16 with me," he said.

Everyone stood and dutifully flipped to the relevant section of the scriptures. This time it was even harder for me to stand motionless, as my knees fluttered unsteadily from the pleasurable sensations radiating inside me.

"It is written..." I tried to read along. "That you shall be holy, for I am holy."

I saw Hannah's hands moving once again inside her prayer book, and suddenly I felt the *other* end of the U-shaped vibrator buzzing against my clit.

"And now Galatians 5:16," Father Fife instructed, barely giving me a chance to recover.

I flipped to the new citation and gasped for breath as my legs wobbled beneath me.

"But I say," I panted unsteadily. "Walk by the Spirit, and you will not gratify the desires of the flesh."

"So it is written," Father Fife said, closing his Bible. "Be righteous as the Lord, and you shall join him in Heaven for everlasting days. And now," he said, magnifying my torture. "I would like us to sing together one of my favorite hymns celebrating His blessing, *Amazing Grace*. Please pick up your hymn books and turn to page forty-three."

"Amazing grace, how sweet the sound," the priest began to sing as the entire congregation joined him in harmony.

"That saved a wretch like me," I sang along, trying to ignore the message that seemed targeted directly at me. As I tried to hold the melody, Hannah cupped the remote-control device in her hand and turned the flywheel to its maximum setting.

"I once was lost, but now am found," I hyperventilated, pressing my legs together as hard as I could to stifle the rising passion that threatened to overtake me.

"Was blind, but now I see," I squealed, singing the last

word decidedly off-pitch as Father Fife turned to see my entire body shaking as I belted the famous hymn.

By the time I'd finished the song, I'd somehow managed to keep it together and fight off the cresting passion that had threatened to put me over the edge. When we finally sat back down, Hannah mercifully turned the vibrator off, and I spread my hands over my ruffled skirt to signal that I'd managed to keep myself composed.

When the service was over and we walked up the aisle behind the rest of the assembly to exit the church, I couldn't wait to get out of the building to wash myself off, figuratively and literally. I was glad that we were at the back of the crowd so nobody could see the back of my skirt. I wasn't sure if my leaking pussy had left a stain, but I sure as hell didn't want one of the parishioners pointing it out. When we finally exited the entrance doors, Father Fife turned to the two of us and smiled.

"I noticed you seemed a little more passionate than usual reciting today's passages, Jade" he said to me.

"Yes, Father," I said, shaking his hand unsteadily. "I felt truly embodied by the spirit."

"And *you*, Hannah," he nodded. "Did you enjoy today's service also?"

"Oh yes," she said. "It was the most moving sermon I've attended in a long time."

"I hope you'll both come again," Father Fife said to the two of us.

"I'm sure we *will*, Father," Hannah smiled as we continued down the steps.

*Like the second we get back home*, I thought to myself, dying to tear off my clothes and squirt all over Hannah's face while she ate out my still-dripping pussy.

**4**

———

"So what did you think?" Hannah said once we got in the car. "Did you find the experience uplifting?"

"I think you're *evil*," I said, reaching under my dress and pulling the vibrator out of my pussy. "You know we're both going to *hell* for that."

"At least we'll know how to enjoy ourselves once we get there," Hannah smirked.

"So, did I pass the test?" I said, inspecting the toy that had caused me so much torture minutes earlier.

"That was pretty impressive," Hannah nodded. "I particularly enjoyed watching you try to finish singing Amazing Grace."

"I practically burst a gasket during that one. Especially when Father Fife looked in my direction."

"That was fucking hilarious," Hannah laughed. "I loved his comment about how *moved* you seemed by the service. I still can't believe he didn't suspect any foul play."

"Maybe he *did*, but he was too embarrassed to admit it. Either way, I'll never be able to show my face again in this church after that little stunt. If *he* doesn't strike me down, then surely the Lord on high will."

"But it was worth it though, right?" Hannah said, angling out of the church parking lot. "It was insanely hot watching you shudder and squirm during the prayers and recitals. Didn't you find it incredibly exciting trying to control yourself in public?"

"How can you be so sure I *did*?" I said, flexing the U-shaped vibrator in my hands. "Maybe I experienced my own little rapture when you weren't looking."

"Oh *please*," Hannah said, stopping at the turnoff to my subdivision. "You don't think I *know* you by now after all the times we've made love? You were never good at hiding your orgasms. Besides your noisy vocalizations, you have a distinct way of contorting your body when you come. Not to mention the tidal wave you produce after a long buildup. Father Fife would have had to send in *Noah's Ark* to save all the believers once you opened the floodgates."

"Speaking of..." I said, placing my hand between her legs as she pulled into my driveway. "If you don't finish what you started, I'm going to spring a leak. Now be a good girl while I sit on your face."

Hannah and I rushed upstairs, where it only took a few seconds for me to pop off while she sucked my aching clit into her mouth. After we both came hard reliving the excitement of the church experience, we flopped back down onto the bed, giggling like two little girls.

"Thanks," I panted. "I needed that."

"That was pretty crazy, wasn't it?" she said. "I still can't believe we got away with it. Front row seat and all."

I rolled over onto my side and propped my head on my elbow as I peered into her eyes.

"It's pretty hard to imagine how you'll be able to step it up after that. What could possibly be harder than trying to hide having sex in a church?"

"Actually, if you think about it, that was almost too easy. After all, hardly anybody was looking at you the whole time. Everybody was focused on the priest or their prayer books. All you had to do was bite your lip and squeeze your legs together under your dress. At the *next* venue, people are going to have a harder time keeping their eyes off of you."

"Why?" I said, darting my eyes over her face trying to imagine what she was scheming. "Are you going to have me sing karaoke or put me in a wet t-shirt contest or something?"

"Not quite," she smiled. "But those aren't bad ideas. No, this next time you're going to be in a public library."

"That doesn't sound so difficult," I said, pulling back. "Everybody will be busy reading a book or searching the stacks."

"Oh, they'll be searching the *stacks* alright," she said, peering down at my plump breasts. "The way I'm going to have you dressed, not many people will be focused on *reading*. Plus, this time there won't be the sound of the preacher's voice or the congregation's singing to cover up your moans and groans. It'll be quiet as a mouse in there."

"Okay..." I said, trying to imagine myself in this new setting. "But where will you be this time?"

"I'll be at an adjacent table, providing a whole *different* kind of kind of distraction."

"No problem," I huffed. "I'll just close my eyes and think about dead cats or something."

"Uh-uh," Hannah said, shaking her head and blinking her eyes at me playfully. "You've got to be fully present in the moment if you want to prove you can control yourself. The whole point of these public displays is for you to show that you can turn it on and off as easily as you said you could."

"Fine," I said. "But you keep adding all these restrictions. What *other* ground rules do I need to know about?"

"You just need to look at me for the duration of the test. *All* of me—both what's going on above and below the table. And you have to remain upright in your seat the whole time. No slouching and trying to hide your best assets."

"You're such a *tease!*" I said, leaning in to bite her nipples. "How long do I have to do this? You can't possibly torture me any longer than the hour you just put me through at the church service."

Hannah cradled my head and wiggled her body down until we made eye contact again.

"Since we'll be ramping up the *other* sources of distraction, I suppose it's only fair that we cut down on the length of this test. Do you think you can survive a half hour without coming?"

"*Pshaw!*" I snorted. "After the church experience, this'll be a cakewalk. When were you thinking of doing this?"

Hannah paused for a moment to consider her options.

"The libraries are busiest on the weekends, but we don't want too many distractions stealing attention away from your performance. How about Wednesday afternoon around three in the afternoon? There should be just enough mid-day traffic around that time to keep everybody amused."

"You're on!" I said, rolling on top of her, pressing my mound against her pussy. "But you don't mind if I try to build up my immunity before then, do you? I figure the more cums I can get in ahead of time, the easier it will be to stem the floodwaters."

"By all means," she said, spreading her legs and tilting her hips until our clits touched. "I want to enjoy living out the fantasy as much as *you* do."

---

On the day of the library visit, Hannah came over to my place an hour early to supervise my preparation. She wanted to make sure I was dressed provocatively enough to attract the attention of the library visitors, both male and female. After trying on a variety of outfits, she finally settled on a tight-fitting tube-top and miniskirt with no underwear. Although my naughty parts were covered up by the opaque fabric, my ample-sized tits and curvy hips left little to the imagination as to what was underneath. This time, I'd be letting it all hang out for everyone to see.

When we got to the library, Hannah found an open table for me to sit in the main atrium, then she positioned herself at an adjacent table about ten feet away. I found a thick text-book resting on the counter and I pulled it over in front of me, hoping to block the view of my pointy tits protruding out of my stretchy tube top. At first, the library was thinly populated, and I shook my head impatiently, wondering what was keeping her from getting started. I was eager to complete the test before it got too busy, but she simply smiled back at me, spreading her legs slowly to reveal her bald pussy. She'd obviously scoped out the place ahead of time, and I scowled at her for making my task even more difficult.

Within ten minutes or so, the library began to fill up as students and office workers began to flit in after class and work hours. A pretty co-ed took a seat kitty-corner to me at my table, while a young stud in an expensive suit plopped some law books down on the table next to Hannah. Whether he was more interested in securing a position to see *me* better or to be next to Hannah, was unclear. Either way, both of them would have prime viewing access to me from their positions.

After tapping out a few messages on their phones, the two visitors opened their books and lowered their heads to begin reading. Within seconds, I felt the familiar tremble of the vibrator fluttering inside me, and I jumped in surprise. The pretty co-ed peered up at me with pinched eyebrows and I turned the page in my encyclopedia, pretending to be absorbed in my reading material. Suddenly, I felt the buzzing sensation of the *internal* branch of the vibrator turn to maximum and I jerked my head up to stare at Hannah in protest. She shook her head disapprovingly, while motioning with her two fingers to keep my gaze focused on her.

I nodded in capitulation, and she dimmed the vibration setting back to low. The well-dressed lawyer occasionally glanced up at me, darting his eyes back and forth between my tight bosom and my bare knees under the table. Hannah smiled when she recognized his attention as she toggled the remote control vibration settings in the palm of her hand.

While the pleasurable sensations began to spread over my pelvic region, I struggled to keep myself still in my seat watching Hannah's slit widening as she spread her legs further apart. When she suddenly turned on the clitoral vibration setting, I emitted a little squeak, and the young blonde girl looked up at me, pursing her lips to say "*Shhh!*"

"Sorry," I whispered, rubbing my hand over my exposed belly. "I've got a bit of an upset stomach."

She shook her head and returned to reading her book. But the direct stimulation on my clit had dramatically

increased my pleasure and my knees began to part unconsciously. The handsome hunk looked up from his law books
when he noticed the movement and peered under the table
as I struggled to keep my knees from fluttering in
excitement.

Hannah noticed the dynamic going on between the two
of us, and when the hunk temporarily looked back down,
she reached into the pocket of her dress and pulled out a
long rubber dildo. As I watched her with glassy eyes, she
slowly inserted the dong into her snatch and began to
stroke it in and out of her hole. I shook my head at her to
show my anger at her tormenting me, but she smiled back
at me, sensuously licking her lips. She knew how much I
liked to trib using a double-sided dildo, and as she rocked
her hips slowly under the table, she took her hand off the
shaft while the other end wobbled tantalizing in my
direction.

I mouthed the words *Fuck You*, and she responded by
saying *Yes Please*. As much as I tried to resist it, as she began
to increase the speed of the clitoral massager, my legs
continued to spread apart with a mind of their own. Before
long, the handsome lawyer looked up at me again, this time
his gaze squarely focused between my legs.

I knew he could probably see me just as well as I could
see Hannah an equal distance away, and his eyes widened
when he saw the strange blue device planted between my
legs. Suddenly, he brought his hand under the table to
adjust himself, and I noticed his pole tenting in his pants. As
his lengthening hard-on snaked up the front of his hips, I
dribbled down the side of my legs, admiring his impressive
package. I grunted unconsciously watching his visceral reac-
tion, and the pretty co-ed sitting next to me looked up again,
shaking her head.

"Why don't you go to the *washroom* if you're not feeling well?" she said. "This is a library!"

"I'm sorry," I said, clutching my stomach. "I think it's something I ate. I'll be finished my research soon, then I'll leave."

The girl looked at my trembling tummy suspiciously, then returned to reading her book. When I peered over again at the hunky lawyer, I saw that he'd unzipped his pants, with his large dick poking straight up toward the underside of his table. Nobody else could have seen what he was doing from my vantage point, and he smiled at me as I spread my legs wider apart in sympathy. Part of me wanted to close my knees and hide the vibrator rumbling inside me, but when I saw him reach under the table and begin to stroke his cock, I couldn't help groaning as I imagined myself planted on top of him.

The girl looked up again, but seeing the strange look on my face as I peered at the hunk across the aisle, she traced my gaze over to him and gasped when she saw what he was doing under the table. After pausing for a moment, she looked back at me and smiled as she lowered her arm under the table and began to move her hand between her legs. I glanced over at Hannah and saw the big rubber dildo glistening from her juices while she watched the three-way action that was happening between our two tables.

As much as I tried to ignore the rising passion emanating from my twitching pussy, it was impossible to avoid the sight of the three beauties stimulating themselves while they watched me squirm and moan with the U-shaped vibrator stimulating every part of my dripping crotch. As the handsome hunk began jerking himself more forcefully under the table, my gaze shifted back to the pretty

co-ed, whose cheeks were beginning to flush from the pleasure she was experiencing under the table. With the four of
us nearing a mutual crescendo, I suddenly flashed back to
my childhood, when my grandmother used to read bedtime
stories to me.

*Goodnight moon*, I said to myself, trying to remember the
words to my favorite story in an effort to shift my focus away
from erotic scene unfolding before me. *Good night, cow
jumping over the moon.*

When I refocused my gaze, I saw Hannah slumping in
her chair with her legs spread wide apart, reaming herself
with two hands tightly gripped around the shaft of the glistening dildo.

*Good night kittens, good night mittens*, I said to myself,
trying to think of anything other than the sight of these
three hotties rimming themselves in the middle of the
public library. Whether each of them was fully aware of
what the other was doing, from my perspective the sight of
them pleasuring themselves together was impossible to
resist.

I glanced at the pretty co-ed, and she looked me straight
in the eye as a bright flush spread over her cheeks. When I
turned back toward the hunky lawyer, he suddenly stopped
moving his hand as he gripped his purple crown in his fist,
spewing long ropes of cum all over the underside of the
table.

*Good night, bear. Good night, chairs*, I murmured quickly
under my breath.

When the girl saw the guy spurting cum out of his huge
dick, she hunched over and gasped, jerking rhythmically in
her seat. Seeing the other two coming so hard only a few
feet away from me, Hannah groaned softly as she pulled the

rubber dildo deep into her pussy, flapping her knees uncontrollably.

*Good night, stars. Good night, air. Good night, noises everywhere*, I said, feeling my juices streaming steadily down the insides of my legs.

## 5

"**N**o *fair!*" I protested when Hannah and I left the library. "You get to have all the fun while I suffer in silence!"

"I never said *I* couldn't come while you were doing these tests," Hannah smiled. "That's half the attraction. Nothing turns me on more than watching you twist and squirm while I stimulate you from a distance."

"*Give* me that fucking thing," I said, tearing the remote control device from her hand. "I don't want to wait another second to get off."

"Right *here*?" Hannah said, looking around the library entrance at the passing patrons.

"Why not? I've already had sex in two public places. What difference will it make if I do it *outside*?"

I peered around me and saw a small alcove near an emergency exit behind a stand of bushes.

"There's a relatively secluded spot over there. You can be my lookout."

"Fuck that," Hannah said, grabbing my hand, pulling me behind the hedge. "I want a piece of this too."

We ducked into the doorway, pressing our bodies together and I flicked on the remote control switch. Hannah reached down and pulled the vibrator out of my pussy, then reinserted each end into our separate holes.

"There's more than *one* way to use this flexible toy," she smiled.

"Except *this* time," I said, "I'll be in charge of controlling the level of stimulation."

I tapped the two buttons on the controller then adjusted the flywheels to their maximum setting. Hannah lifted the front of our skirts and pressed her mound against mine, kissing me passionately. Even though I only had half of the U-shaped vibrator throbbing against me, the action of Hannah's mound grinding up against my own provided more than enough clitoral stimulation. As we thrust our tongues into each other's mouths, I reached under Hannah's dress and grabbed her buttocks, pulling her hard against me.

"I'm going to cum all over your little twat," I said, feeling my orgasm rising within me like a powerful volcano.

"Let it go, girl," Hannah said.

I lifted my knee and wrapped my leg around her ass, pointing my vulva against her mound.

"Uhnn," I groaned. "Here it comes. *Fuckkkk!*"

As my pussy clamped down over the fat end of the vibrator, I squirted my pent-up juices out the sides of my slit all over Hannah's abdomen as we shook in each other's arms from the combined stimulation of the curved wand.

"*Fuck me,*" Hannah said as we collapsed against the side of the door with our juices streaming down the insides of our legs. "I never even thought about using this as a double-sided dildo."

"How do *you* like not being in control for a change?" I

said, raising my eyebrows in protest. "Now you know what I've been going through these last two episodes."

"I have a whole new respect for what you've been able to accomplish," she nodded. "Especially with those two hotties jerking off right next to you."

"You have no idea," I said. "That hunk sitting next to you was hung like a horse. You should have seen him when he finally dumped his load. I thought he'd never stop coming underneath the desk."

"I guess the clean-up crew will have more than a few wads of gum to scrape of the bottom of the table next time," Hannah chuckled. "But I was more focused on the cute girl sitting beside you. She certainly changed her tune when she finally figured out what was going on."

"When I saw the sex flush roll over her cheeks, it took every ounce of my willpower not to come along with her."

"How *did* you manage to keep it together?" Hannah asked. "I thought you were really going to lose control this time."

"I just transported myself somewhere else and tried to think of something as far removed from my predicament as possible."

"Well, whatever it was, it seemed to work. Though I dare say the three of *us* more than made up for your lack of enthusiasm. I haven't come that hard in ages."

"So what now?" I said. "Now that I've managed to get the hotel and airfare paid for, what do I have to do to cover the meals for our trip to Bora Bora?"

Hannah pulled the vibrator out of our pussies and leaned against the opposite wall of the alcove as she looked at me with a sly smile.

"We have to step it *up* another notch, right? Both of these times you were fully clothed and had a few props to distract attention from what was going on down there. This next time, you're going to be completely *naked*."

I shook my head and peered at her with a quizzical look.

"Are you taking me to a nude beach or something?"

"Even better," she smirked. "You're going to be a nude model for a college art class."

"What the–" I gasped, feeling my pussy twitch one last time, sending another stream of juices running down my leg.

---

For the next week or so, all I could think about was what it would be like to stand in front of a group of strangers while they sketched me in the nude. As much as I tried to get more details from Hannah, she refused to give me any more information until we arrived at the studio. I wasn't exactly sure how she was going to pull off stimulating me from a distance with a vibrator sticking out of my pussy. But every time I thought about it, I stood in front of my full-length dressing mirror imagining everyone watching me while I jilled myself to orgasm.

On the scheduled appointment day, Hannah drove me to the local college, where we met with the art professor to go over the ground rules for the session. The prof was younger and prettier than I imagined, and I sat in rapt attention while she explained how it all worked.

"Hi, I'm Danielle," she said, introducing herself to the two of us.

"Jade," I said, extending my hand.

"Hannah," my partner-in-crime said.

"Which one of you will be posing today?"

I held up my hand meekly.

"I'm just here for moral support," Hannah smiled.

"The protocol is pretty straight-forward," Danielle said. "We'll keep you covered up until everyone is ready to begin. Then I'll ask you to hold a pose for about thirty minutes while the students draw you in the nude. I'll be circulating around the room during this time, offering feedback and critique on their compositions. The most important thing is for you to try to remain as still as possible for the duration of the assignment."

While she was talking to the two of us, I stole occasional glances at her figure. She was wearing a tight-fitting mid-length skirt and a white cotton blouse partially unbuttoned at the neck. Her breasts were full and round, and my gaze kept falling to her sexy cleavage and her toned legs crossed at the knee. By the time she finished her briefing, I could feel the heat emanating from my throbbing pussy.

"Did you have any questions?" she asked.

"How many people are we expecting to show up?" I asked nervously.

"We have twenty students in my class, and I expect most of them to show up for this assignment. This is one of the more popular electives."

"I can see why," Hannah said, eyeing my curvy figure under my robe.

"And I can't cover up any part of my body?" I said.

"That's the whole point of figure drawing," Danielle said. "To sketch the subject in his or her full glory."

"Don't people sometimes get–um–*excited* with so many eyes on their naked body?" I said, wondering especially how a male model would manage to keep himself composed in this situation.

"I tell both the models and the artists that it's perfectly

normal and natural. That's part of the challenge–to capture their feelings and emotions in a still composition."

"May I participate in the session also?" Hannah asked. "I mean as an *artist*. I've always wanted to sketch Jade in the nude."

"Of course," Danielle said. "I only ask that you try not to distract the model with any overt comments or expressions."

"I wouldn't *dream* of it," Hannah smiled.

"Okay," the professor said. "Why don't you take a few minutes to freshen up and prepare yourself while the students get set up?"

Hannah and I walked out into the hallway where we found a private washroom, locking the door behind us.

"Okay," I said, crossing my arms impatiently. "How exactly are you going to pull this off with everyone staring at my naked pussy?"

"Never fear, my pretty," Hannah cooed, taking a small dumbbell-shaped object out of her purse. "These are a special type of Ben-wa balls. They vibrate in different ways, depending on how I adjust the controller. Everything's going to be hiding *inside* you this time. No one will be any the wiser as to what's going on, unless you give them reason to suspect otherwise."

"Ben-wa balls," I nodded, reflecting back on the time I'd used them in the airplane lavatory with my Swedish stewardess friends. "Ingenious."

"You shouldn't have any trouble controlling yourself with *these* things, right?" Hannah said, raising a playful eyebrow. "Only one *part* of you is going to be stimulated this time."

"Well, as you've explained to me many times, the main body of my clitoris is actually located on the *inside* of my vagina, not the outside. And I've already had some experience with these things. So *no*, it's not going to be any easier to control myself."

"Well this should be all the more interesting then," Hannah smiled, reaching under my robe and inserting the chrome balls into my slit.

When we returned to the studio, the classroom had already filled up with students, and the instructor motioned for everyone to take their seats. There was an even mix of men and women, and they were all young and cute. As Danielle introduced me to the class, I scanned around the room, feeling my pussy throb as I made eye contact with each student.

In the front row, a pretty brunette with a cute ponytail smiled at me as I glanced at her tawny thighs exposed in cut-off jeans under her tilted drafting table. Directly behind her, a cute redhead with little freckles sprinkled over her nose peered up at me, gazing at my excited nipples poking two darts in the soft fabric of my robe. As I traced a line further toward the back of the room, I saw an African-American man looking like a young Denzel Washington nodding at me as he admired my curvy figure.

*Fuck me*, I thought. *They're not going to make this any easier for me.*

As I imagined fucking each one of them in turn, the professor interrupted my thoughts with final instructions to the group.

"Because of the personal nature of this session, I'll ask everyone to place their phones in their pockets or purses to protect the privacy of our subject. You all know the protocol for drawing the model, which I've already explained to Jade, so if you'd like to take out your drawing materials now, we can begin. Jade, if you feel comfortable, you may disrobe now and sit comfortably on the stool."

The professor motioned to an adjacent chair, and I pulled off my robe and sat awkwardly on the bench with my feet propped up on the lower bar and my knees clamped tightly together.

"You may wish to turn your body a few degrees to your left," Danielle instructed, "so our students can depict a partial side profile. Try to relax your legs by placing one foot on the floor and the other on the lower foot rest. As far as your hands, most models find it most comfortable to rest them in their lap. Since we'll need you to remain as still as possible for the duration of the session, you may find it useful to find a focal point somewhere in the room where you can fix your gaze. Are we ready to begin?"

I nodded my head and scanned the back wall, seeing a message board above the African-American student's head. A sign listed the ten meeting norms to optimize productivity, and I began to read them quietly to myself to distract attention from the twenty sets of eyes starting at my naked body.

*Show up on time and come prepared*, the first rule said.

*Check*, I said to myself. *Although I'm not sure coming to class with two steel balls embedded in my pussy qualifies exactly as 'prepared'.*

Suddenly, I felt the balls begin to tremble inside me, and I shifted uncomfortably on my chair.

*Stay mentally and physically present*, the second rule said.

I'm physically present alright, but my *mind* is definitely elsewhere.

I drew my focus back about ten feet, noticing the cute brunette in the front row swinging her legs as she slowly etched her pencil over her drawing pad. In my periphery, I could see the white fringes on the bottom of her shorts flapping over her inner thighs, and I wondered if she was doing it to help focus on her drawing, or if it was because she was getting aroused by my naked body.

I could feel my nipples hardening as I watched her hands moving over the canvas, wondering what it would feel like to have her touch my *real* body. Hannah must have noticed my distraction, because I could feel the movement of the Ben-wa balls steadily increasing inside my pussy. Suddenly, I was mindful of how wet the chrome seat under my ass had become, feeling the tip of my clit dip into the little puddle I'd created in the concave surface of the stool. As she dialed up the vibration of the two balls shaking inside me, the radiating forces on the underside of my vulva made little ripples in the fluid, splashing gently back and forth over my tingling bulb.

*Great*, I grimaced. *Just what I need right now. Yet another form of uncontrolled stimulation to my most sensitive body part.*

I was tempted to lower my pinky under my resting palms to stimulate my aching clit, then I remembered the purpose of this exercise was to *contain* my pleasure not encourage it.

*Contribute to the meeting goals*, the third rule on the sign said.

*Check*, I said, clenching my buttock cheeks to fight off the rising passion.

I adjusted my focus to the pretty redhead in the same line of sight and noticed her cheeks flushing over her pale skin. For a moment, I imagined what it would be like to suck on her pretty pussy while I watched a deeper flush roll over her naked chest.

*Get it together Jade*, I said to myself, glancing up at the clock on the wall. *You only need to get through another fifteen minutes, then you can fantasize all you want about fucking these cuties.*

My eyes drifted back to the sign above Denzel Washington's head, reading the fourth rule.

*Let everyone participate*, it instructed.

I peered down a few inches, noticing his arm muscles flexing as he brushed his fingers over his canvas.

*I bet he knows how to please a woman with those soft hands of his*, I fantasized.

Suddenly I felt the two chrome balls begin to flex back and forth, caressing the walls of my dripping pussy. While they pounded inside me, I imagined his cock sliding in and out of my hole as I gripped his powerful arms.

*Fuck, Hannah*, I cursed under my breath. It was almost like she was reading my mind, adjusting the action of the Ben-wa balls to mimic the fantasies that were racing through my mind.

With the pleasurable sensations steadily building inside my womb, I could feel my breathing increasing as my breasts began to rise and fall on my chest. Surely everyone must have noticed my internal distraction, and I half expected the teacher to admonish me to remain still. But she was too busy circulating among the group to pay any attention to me. When she angled back toward the front of the room, she bent over to observe the brunette's work, and I gawked at her fleshy breasts, barely supported by the flimsy fabric of her blouse.

*God damn*, I murmured. *I'd love to bury my face in those tits. Or better yet, rub my cunt against her melons while she watched me squirt all over her body.*

As my body continued to heave unconsciously on my stool, my clit dipped in and out of the increasingly large puddle I was forming on the seat, and I clenched my jaw trying to stifle my rising passion.

I glanced back up at the wall clock and noticed I only

had five minutes left to finish my test. Recognizing my increasing distress, Hannah flicked her thumbs over the remote control and suddenly I felt the Ben-was balls begin to *rotate* on their axis.

*Oh my God*, I panted under my breath. *What else can these evil things do?*

By now, I was being silently fucked by the three-way action of the miniature dumbbells. In addition to flexing back and forth, they were twirling inside me like a slingshot, while rotating rapidly. The combined stimulation on the walls of my pussy was almost unbearable.

I could see my thigh muscles clenching as I stiffened my body trying to fight back the rising wall of pleasure, but just as I was about to pop off, the teacher stood up and told everyone to put their pencils down. Suddenly, the whirring balls stopped moving inside me and I relaxed my buttock muscles, feeling my burning lips dip back down into the warm puddle beneath me.

"Okay everyone," Danielle announced. "Time's up. Please stop sketching and bring your completed compositions to the front of the room before you leave. Jade, you may put on your robe now. Thank you for your time and participation in today's art class. We have a small parting gift for you before you leave. Next week, we have a *sculpture* class scheduled. If you'd like to come back and join us again, we'd love to have you."

I pulled the robe back over my shoulders, then Danielle handed me a long cardboard tube and thanked me again for my participation.

"If you'd like to model for us again, please let me know," she said, clasping my shaking hand. "You seem to have inspired a whole new level of dedication in my students' craft."

Later that day when I got home and opened the tube, I pulled out a long piece of parchment paper. Sketched on the front was a picture of me with my head thrown back in the throes of passion with my hands positioned in front of my snatch between my outspread legs. But instead of the stool I was sitting on in class, I was sitting on a giant, stylized chrome dildo, deeply embedded in my pussy. The signature on the bottom of the sketch simply read *Han*.

I smiled, admiring the surreal illustration.

"I didn't know you could draw, you little devil," I said.

Then I pulled my favorite rabbit vibrator out of my nightstand and rammed it inside me, beginning to dream of what fantasy Hannah had in store for me next.

"I can't *imagine* what you have planned for this final test," I said to Hannah when she came to pick me up a few days later. "What could be more difficult than having to stand motionless for thirty minutes while you stimulate me completely naked in front of twenty sexy college students?"

"That was pretty hot," Hannah nodded. "You definitely earned your choice of five-star restaurants on our little getaway to Bora Bora."

"What's my motivation for this last challenge?" I said. "Everything's already pretty much paid for. What's stopping me from just enjoying myself and letting it all go?"

"How does a snorkeling expedition to swim with the sharks and rays in the crystalline waters of an off-shore reef sound?"

"Not as dangerous as what I suspect you've got cooked up for me today."

"What about a catamaran cruise to our own private island for a candlelight dinner under the stars?"

"That's definitely on my bucket list..."

"Or a full-day spa treatment with hot stone massage, deep-clean facial, and sensuous body scrub?"

"Okay, *fine*, you little bugger," I chuckled. "You've twisted my arm. So, what have you got in store for me today?"

Hannah paused as her mouth curled up on one side.

"Watching you try to recite the prayers while I stimulated you at the church got me thinking. That was almost too *easy* with everyone looking the other way. At this *next* venue, everyone's going to be hanging on your every word..."

"What–am I going to be giving some kind a speech or something?"

"Almost," she smiled. "You're going to be reading a book for some of my book club friends."

"What's the book?"

"Delta of Venus, by Anais Nin."

"I've heard of that," I nodded. "Isn't that the one with all the steamy vignettes describing the author's sexual escapades?"

"Yes."

"So let me get this straight," I said. "You want me to read a story describing graphic sex without getting aroused while you stimulate me from a distance with a secret vibrator?"

"Exactly."

I shook my head, hardly believing the lengths Hannah had gone to to dream up these outrageous scenarios.

"Who will be my audience?"

"It's an LGBT book club, so it'll be a group of about twenty young women–"

"You've *got* to be kidding me," I said. "You expect me to remain composed while I'm reading a sex scene surrounded by a bunch of hot lesbians?"

"If you want the spa and the cruise and the snorkeling expedition..." she smirked.

"You are *truly* an evil witch, you know that, right?"

"That's why you love me so much," Hannah said, rubbing up against me playfully.

"And where exactly is this latest excursion going to take place?" I said, wondering what else she was planning to raise the stakes.

"At the local bookstore. They have a little coffee shop in the back which they allow our group to use from time to time."

"Great," I said, pushing her away in disgust. "So you're going to be diddling me as an untold number of strangers walk in and out of the coffee shop?"

"Mmm-hmm," Hannah nodded.

"Will you be using Ben-wa balls again, since I'll be exposed to the public?"

"Oh *no*," Hannah said, shaking her head teasingly. "We'll have to make this a little more interesting if you want to pass the ultimate test."

"You've already subjected me to the dual action of the *We-Vibe* vibrator. What could possibly be more stimulating than that?"

Hannah reached into her purse and pulled out a familiar finger-shaped toy.

"Not the *Osé* vibrator!" I squealed. "You're making this almost impossible! How do you expect me to control myself with a realistic finger and tongue caressing my private parts while I'm getting turned on reading a sexy story to a bunch of sexy women?"

"*You're* the one who bragged about how easily you can turn it on and off," Hannah shrugged. "If you pass this final test, I'll give you whatever you want."

"If I pass this test," I said, crossing my arms indignantly, "I'll expect Scarlett Johansson as my personal masseuse and Thomas Keller as our chef!"

"I'll see what I can arrange..."

---

W hen we got to the bookstore, Hannah set me up on a comfortable settee with a small reading table. On its surface rested a hardcover book with an image of a half-naked woman kneeling on an upholstered chair with her legs splayed in a sexy pose.

*At least I'll be reasonably covered up this time*, I thought, beginning to get aroused looking at the provocative picture.

Hannah had allowed me to wear a loose-fitting summer dress that concealed most of my body, but she'd insisted I go au naturel underneath to permit maximum freedom of movement for both me and the vibrator. As the book club members began to wander into the bookstore, she introduced me to each one in turn, and I was struck by how young and pretty they all were. It was far cry from the collection of frumpy nerds I'd half-expected. When everybody had assembled in the lounge, she stood up to address the group while I tried to compose myself by straightening out my dress over my shaking knees.

"Welcome to the monthly meeting of the Literary Coven book group," Hannah said. "Today I've invited a special guest to read a passage from one of my favorite erotic books, Delta of Venus, by Anais Nin. She's kindly, um, *volunteered* to read a chapter I think you'll find quite stimulating and moving. So without any further ado, I give you my friend, Jade."

The women clapped softly while they examined my

naked shoulders and legs as I smiled back at them politely. I shifted my weight to the edge of the settee and picked up the book, turning to the bookmarked chapter, titled *Elena*.

*The three women met*, I read softly, *driven inside the same cafe on a day of heavy rain...*

I had no idea when Hannah would begin her private stimulation of me and the anticipation made the reading all the more tension-filled.

*Leila, perfumed and dashing, carrying her head high, a silver fox stole undulating around her shoulders over her trim black suit...*

What beautiful prose, I thought to myself, already beginning to lose myself in the story.

*Elena, in a wine-colored velvet, and Bijou, in her streetwalker's costume, which she could never abandon, the tight-fitting black dress and high-heeled shoes.*

Interesting premise, I said to myself. I was already hooked, beginning to understand the attraction of sharing a well-written book with a collection of like-minded women. I glanced over at Hannah, who was peering at me with a devilish look in her eyes.

Suddenly, I felt the long finger of the Osé vibrator beginning to flex inside my pussy, and I squirmed on my seat trying to distract myself from the humanlike sensation.

*Leila smiled at Bijou*, I said, pausing to collect my breath, *then recognized Elena. Shivering, the three of them sat down before aperitifs.*

As I continued reading the story, Hannah slowly ramped up the vibration of the undulating finger caressing the walls of my pussy while I struggled to maintain my composure.

*What Elena had not expected*, I shuddered, *was to be completely intoxicated with Bijou's voluptuous charm. On her right sat Leila, incisive, brilliant, and on her left, Bijou, like a bed of sensuality Elena wanted to fall into.*

While I read the exquisitely written book, I found myself getting increasingly pulled into the story, imagining myself in the role of Elena, surrounded by the two fascinating women. When the story took a sexy turn, I found my body reacting as if I were right there with them.

*The first one to move was Leila,* I read, looking up to see a pretty blonde staring squarely into my eyes. *Who slid her jeweled hand under Bijou's skirt and gasped slightly with surprise at the unexpected touch of flesh where she had expected to find silky underwear.*

I paused for a moment to take a drink of water. The group nodded at me softly, recognizing my silent torment.

*Leila had a moment of jealousy,* I read, gulping down the last bit of water in my mouth. *Each caress she gave to Bijou, Bijou transmitted to Elena–the very same caress.*

I jerked suddenly in my seat and closed my eyes, feeling the pleasurable sensations from the undulating wand beginning to wash over me.

"Sorry," I said, looking up. "I guess I'm getting more attached to this story than I expected."

"Don't worry," one of the girls whispered. "We're enjoying your rendition. We've never had someone read a book so...*passionately.*"

I peered over at Hannah, who was looking at me with a wicked grin. I cleared my throat, feeling the lips of my vulva moistening with a light dew.

*After Leila kissed Bijou's luxuriant mouth,* I read, turning the page, *Bijou took Elena's lips between her own. When Leila's hand slipped further under Bijou's dress*–huh! I gasped, feeling a wave of pleasure roll over me–*Bijou slid her hand under*

*Elena's. Elena, seeing Bijou offered, dared to touch her voluptuous body, following every contour of her rich curves...*

As I continued reading the erotic story, my hips began to move unconsciously on the dimpled settee, mimicking the action of the characters in the story. I could feel the moisture beginning to pour out of me as the pendulous finger probed deep inside my hole. Coffee shop patrons paused briefly to peer over at me, pinching their eyebrows trying to imagine why I was so immersed in the story.

*A bed of down, soft, firm flesh without bones*, I read haltingly, *smelling of sandalwood and musk. Her own nipples hardened as she touched Bijou's breasts.*

Suddenly I became aware of how the *rest* of my body was responding as I read the sexy tale. With my bare nipples rubbing against the soft cotton fabric of my dress, every hair on my body was standing on end, as goose bumps covered every square inch of my skin.

*When her hand passed around Bijou's buttocks*–huh, huh, huh, I spasmed quietly on the sofa–*it met Leila's hand.*

At this point I still only had the internal part of the vibrator moving against me, and I shuddered to think how I would keep it together if and when Hannah turned on the other half of the device. As the action in the story continued to ramp up, so did the pleasure continuing to build unabated in my twitching pussy.

*Leila began to undress*, I panted, *exposing a soft little black satin corselet, which held her stockings with tiny black garters. Her thighs...slender and white, gleamed...her sex lay in shadow.*

*Fuck me*, I thought, picturing the scene like I was right there. *This is an incredibly erotic story. To hell with reading this in public–as soon as I get home, I'm going to rip off my clothes and enjoy this properly in the privacy of my own bedroom.*

Hannah suddenly peered up at me, reading my thoughts, and I felt the snake-like appendage hidden in the *other* end of the vibrator begin to press up against my burning clit.

*Oh God*, I panted under my breath, trying to steel myself against the rising passion beginning to consume my body.

*Leila pressed Bijou onto her side*, I hissed, *with one leg thrown over Leila's shoulder. And she was kissing Bijou between her*–uhn–*legs.*

While I read the increasingly bawdy scene, my face contorted in a series of pained expressions as I tried to ignore the animatronic appendages caressing both sides of my pussy.

*Now and then...Bijou jerked backwards...away from the stinging kisses and bites, the tongue that was as hard as a man's sex.*

Hannah must have chosen this passage explicitly, knowing how much it would torture me to read a passage mirroring the action of the device whirring and shaking against my vulva. As I continued reading the story, she modulated the type and intensity of the device's movement to match precisely how the characters were interacting.

*With her hands, Elena had been enjoying the shape of Bijou's body, and now she inserted her finger into the tight little aperture...*

I groaned out loud, feeling the disembodied finger beginning to caress the front of my G-spot.

*There she could feel*, I moaned, *every contraction caused by Leila's kisses*–uhn–*as if she were touching the wall against which Leila moved her tongue.*

As the fleshy tongue of the Osé vibrator rolled over my tingling clit, I felt myself beginning to lose control. The wall of pleasure rising within me was like a riptide, pushing back against my feeble attempt to resist the flow.

*When she was about to come and could no longer defend herself against her pleasure*—uh, uh, I heaved—*Leila stopped kissing her, leaving Bijou halfway on the peak of an excruciating sensation, half-crazed.*

Recognizing that I was on the verge of coming, Hannah simultaneously stopped the vibrator, and I looked up at her with a start.

*Please*, I mouthed to her, asking her to release me from my torment. She held up her finger up and twirled it in circles, instructing me to finish the chapter. I closed my eyes, taking a deep breath, and resumed reading.

*Uncontrollable now*, I gasped, *like some magnificent maniac, Bijou threw herself over Elena's body, parted her legs, placed herself between them, glued her sex to Elena's and moved, moved with desperation.*

*Yes*, I whispered softly, desperate to consummate my own pleasure along with my new imaginary friends.

*Elena was now in the frenzy before climax*, I cackled, feeling both parts of the vibrator starting up inside me again. *She felt a hand under her, a hand she could rub against. She wanted to throw herself on it until it made her come, but she also wanted to prolong her pleasure.*

Hannah turned down the motion of the finger thrusting inside me again, and I cursed her under my breath.

*So she ceased moving, but the hand pursued her*, I grunted. *She stood up, and the hand again traveled towards her sex...*

Possessed of another spirit, I slowly rose out of my chair, cradling the book in two hands as streams of lubrication trickled down the inside of my thighs below the hem of my dress.

*Then she felt Bijou standing against her back, panting. She felt the pointed breasts, the brushing of Bijou's sexual hair against her buttocks.*

As I read the captivating text, my *own* body began to sway and undulate against my literary lover.

*Bijou rubbed against her, knowing the friction would force Elena to turn so as to feel this on her breasts, sex, and belly. Elena's body was so burning hot that she feared one more touch would set off the explosion. Leila sensed this, and the two of them together attacked Bijou, intent on drawing from her the ultimate sensation.*

*Fuck yes*, I panted out loud.

*She was begging now to be satisfied, spread her legs, sought to satisfy herself by friction against the others' bodies. With tongues and fingers, they pried into her, back and front, sometimes stopping to touch each other's tongue—Elena and Leila, mouth to mouth, tongues curled together, over Bijou's spread legs.*

"*Oh God*", I squealed, feeling my climax beginning to overtake me. *Fuck the massage and the snorkeling expedition*, I said to myself. *I need to be taken right now.*

As I read the final passage of the chapter, my hips began to shake while I struggled to hold the book in my hands.

*Bijou's orgasm came like an exquisite torment*, I read. *At each spasm, she moved as if she were being stabbed.*

Suddenly, the walls of my pussy clamped down hard and I gushed like a waterfall onto the hard wooden floor beneath me. Every one of the book club members gasped, realizing what was happening to me, then silence filled the room as I stood trembling in the throes of the most powerful orgasm I could remember.

When I finally put the book down, I looked up at them meekly. They stared at me for a long moment, still in shock at what they'd just witnessed, then they all stood up, clapping loudly in unison. As I smiled back at them, feeling the cool sticky moisture between my legs, I glanced over at Hannah and she nodded toward me, joining the others in applause.

I shook my head in amazement, realizing I'd earned every piece of her promised prize.

THE
*Dinner*
PARTY
AN EROTIC ADVENTURE
VICTORIA RUSH

*Everybody's an exhibitionist in disguise...*

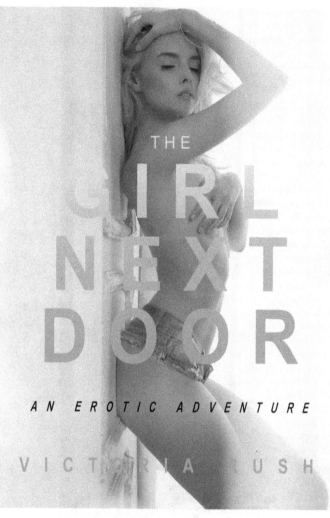

# THE
# GIRL
# NEXT
# DOOR

## *AN EROTIC ADVENTURE*

## VICTORIA RUSH

*Spying on the neighbors just got a lot more interesting...*

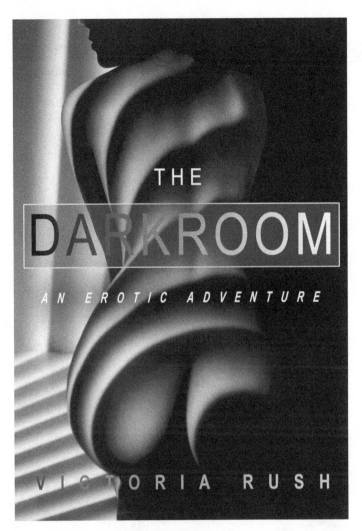

# THE
# DARKROOM

## *AN EROTIC ADVENTURE*

*VICTORIA RUSH*

*Everything's sexier in the dark...*

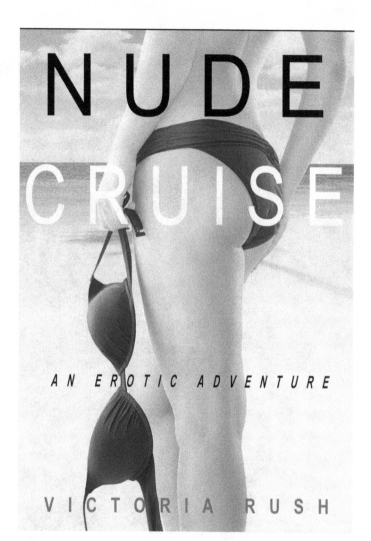

# NUDE
# CRUISE

## AN EROTIC ADVENTURE

### VICTORIA RUSH

*Some people get wet on a cruise for different reasons...*

*Books 1 -5 in the bestselling series - 60% off*

# THE DINNER PARTY - PREVIEW
### FINGER FOOD

S ometime later, I heard a soft tap on my bedroom door. Not wanting to remove myself just yet from my cocoon of luxury, I called out to answer.

"Yes?"

"It's time for your massage," a woman's voice replied.

"Just one minute please."

I reluctantly stepped out of the bath and quickly toweled myself dry. I wrapped a large bath sheet around me, re-donned my mask, then opened the bedroom door.

A petite young Asian girl greeted me, wearing a kimono similar to mine and a crimson masquerade mask.

Apparently not everybody who works here always walks around stark naked.

The girl was utterly breathtaking. Long jet-black hair cascaded over high cheekbones past pouty lips, her delicate collarbones peeking from the top of her kimono. I could see her breasts and hips outlined by the tightly-wrapped kimono and suddenly wished that she too had come to my boudoir naked.

"My name is Jasmine," she said. "I'm your personal

masseuse and esthetician. Are you ready for your final preparation?

Just the thought of this beauty laying her tender hands on me sent a shiver down my spine.

"Definitely. Please come in. How would you like me to prepare?"

"Come with me, please."

Jasmine led me into the bathroom, where she nonchalantly removed her kimono and hung it behind the bathroom door.

*Oh my God.*

I didn't think anyone in this place could get more beautiful or sensuous. Jasmine had perfectly shaped B-cup breasts with a thin indentation running down the center of her perfectly toned stomach. Like everyone else in this place, her pubis was utterly bald and flawless. She barely looked eighteen and I was just about to ask her age, but she spoke first.

"If you'd like to remove your towel and lay face down on the table, we can get started. May I call you Jade?"

There was something about her confident manner and tone that belied her youthful appearance. I had no inhibitions whatsoever about displaying myself unclothed to this stranger.

"Yes, thank you, Jasmine." I unhooked my bath sheet and threw it against the side of the tub.

"Would you like me to drape your backside?" Jasmine asked.

"That won't be necessary," I quickly answered.

Jasmine walked over to the vanity counter and picked up two small bottles of oil resting under an orange radiant lamp. She brought them back to the massage table, opened one, and poured the oil into one cupped hand then rubbed her hands together. The scent of lavender wafted toward my nose.

I closed my eyes in anticipation of her touch. I'd had massages before, but nothing as sensuous and stimulating as this. When her hands touched the small of my back, I jerked reflexively from the sexual tension. My heart was beating a hundred miles an hour as I felt the blood coursing through my veins.

Jasmine must have sensed my nervous tension and began pressing her fingers more firmly into my back as she moved them slowly up each side of my spine. The warm oil allowed her hands to glide effortlessly across my skin. She used every surface of her hands to massage my muscles, expertly kneading my skin with her fingers and palm.

I began to relax as my muscles softened and surrendered to her touch. She sensuously massaged every part of my back, shoulders, and neck, applying just the right amount of pressure. Periodically, she would pour more warm oil on my lower back, dipping her hands in it to replenish the silky lubrication against my pliant skin.

Just as the sexual tension began to subside from the utter relaxation of the massage, Jasmine moved her hands down to my buttocks and began to caress them in soft circular motions. My glutes contracted involuntarily and I unconsciously pressed my mound into the firm padding of the table. Suddenly I was quickly reminded that a gorgeous young woman was caressing my naked body. She cupped each buttock between her hands as she massaged my ass tantalizingly, her little finger sliding slowly into the cleft just above my anus.

Periodically, I'd partially open one of my eyes with my head turned in her direction to look at her gorgeous body. My head was at the same level as her midsection, and my mouth watered as I watched her stomach muscles flex and her hips undulate with each movement of her hands. At times her pussy was almost right beside me and I wanted to reach out and run my own fingers up her soft legs.

I was in total heaven and getting wetter by the moment. Just when I thought I couldn't stand it anymore, she suddenly moved her hands down to my feet and began massaging her thumbs into my soles.

I'd always loved having my feet massaged, but nobody did it like Jasmine. She cradled my foot and used every part of her hands to massage and knead every surface from my heel to my toes. I didn't want her to stop, but there were other parts of my body that were screaming for attention.

As if reading my thoughts, she began moving her hands up toward my calf, using her thumbs to spread the muscle apart. She lingered almost as long on my calf as she had on my foot, rolling the ball of my calf between both of her hands, sliding her slick hands up and down erotically. I couldn't help imagining how she might use those same hands to massage a man's erect cock in a similar manner. My mind wandered again to what pleasures lay in wait for me over dinner.

After shifting her hands to my right leg and giving my other foot and calf similar attention, she placed each hand just behind my knees and began to slowly move them up towards my buttocks. Her thumbs pressed against my inner thighs as she glided tantalizingly close to my apex.

I rolled my legs outward in an invitation to move closer. My legs were parted enough that I was sure she could see my vulva from her vantage point behind me. In my highly aroused state, my lips were engorged and spread apart, revealing my moist and quivering opening.

But as much as I desperately wanted her to, Jasmine

never touched me there. She repeatedly slid her hands right up to the edge of my slit, pressing and rotating her thumbs on the fleshy meat of my upper thighs just below my aching pussy. I suppose this was part of her master plan—to tease me mercilessly and inflame my passions so I'd be ready for just about anything at the main event.

It was certainly working. After thirty minutes of Jasmine's ministrations, I was grinding my pussy into the table trying desperately to give my clit some needed direct stimulation.

Just when I thought I couldn't be teased any more tantalizingly, Jasmine opened one of the bottles of warm oil and poured it directly into the crack of my ass. She paused as the fluid flowed down and directly over my parted lips. I almost came from the gentle movement of the warm liquid as it trickled across the folds of my labia, channeled toward the junction where they joined together at my clit. I shuddered in pleasure at the feeling, even if it was only the subtlest of touch.

Jasmine suddenly interrupted my thoughts.

"Would you like to turn over now?"

It was the first time she had spoken directly to me since the massage started, and it surprised me in my catatonic, pre-orgasmic state. I practically flipped over like a fish out of water and spread my legs expectantly. Finally, I'd get some relief. Surely, she couldn't leave me hanging like this.

"It's time for your final grooming," she said. "I'll need you to part your legs a bit further to provide full access."

Grooming? I knew this was part of the process, but somehow it didn't seem fair to transition at this precise moment. At least I'd be able to stay on the comfortable massage table instead of the clinical vinyl chairs used by my regular esthetician.

Jasmine walked over to another cabinet by the makeup table and withdrew a leather bag from one of the drawers, then brought it back to the table. She reached into the bag and pulled out a cordless hair trimmer.

"Do you have a preference regarding your appearance?" she asked. "Do you prefer natural, neatly trimmed, or bare?"

I knew she was referring to my pubic hair, which I generally kept neatly trimmed. I'd always thought going fully bald was unnatural and unseemly, catering to men's prurient fantasies of fucking young schoolgirls. But in this situation, it seemed entirely appropriate, like I was stripping away all my camouflage and armor.

If tonight was all about being watched, I might as well bare myself in every sense of the word and truly let my inhibitions go. I began to fantasize about rubbing my bare pussy against Jasmine's while she poured warm oil between us. The more work she had to do on me, the more chance I'd have to make this last and hopefully get off.

I didn't hesitate. "Bare, thank you."

"As you wish," she said. "I'll remove the long hairs first with the trimmer, then shave you smooth with a razor."

No waxing? This was different. I was relieved to not have to bear the painful and violent trial of having my hairs ripped out en masse. Although shaving down there was always a scary proposition, I felt safe in the capable and practiced hands of this beautiful esthetician.

Jasmine nodded, then flipped a switch on the trimmer. The device buzzed softly as she placed it gently on my mound. I had only a light dusting of fur and it didn't take long for her to remove it with a few short strokes over my pubis. I shuddered as the vibrations penetrated deep into my core. If she had placed the flat head on my clitoris, I would have popped off in a millisecond. Instead, she turned the trimmer face-down and gently swiped the vibrating teeth against the sides of my vulva, sensuously separating my labia with her hands as she moved the device between my legs to trim the hairs on the inside and outside of my labia.

It was an insanely titillating feeling, but just clinical enough to bring me down from my plateau and shift my focus. My mind wandered to the upcoming feast, and I contemplated what surprises lay in wait at the main event. The hostesses had suggested there would be 'contact' of some sort during the meal, and I was intrigued exactly who and how it would be administered. The idea of being fully bald, cleansed, and thoroughly stimulated going into the event was an incredible rush.

Jasmine continued with the trimmer all the way down my perineum to my anus, barely touching me with the trimmer so as not to pinch any delicate tissues. Apparently there were no parts of my erogenous zone that would remain untouched, now—and perhaps later.

She turned off the trimmer and placed it at the foot of the table. Then she took a bottle of gel from the bag and spread the gel on her hands. Using both hands, she spread it gently between my legs, starting on my mound all the way down to my rosebud.

My body almost levitated above the table as Jasmine finally laid her hands directly on my clitoris. The gel had a mild stinging quality that added to the stimulating sensation. If this was meant to excite my follicles in preparation for the shave, it wasn't the only feature of my anatomy that it made erect. I could feel the hood of my clitoris retract as my button filled with blood and began to push outward. Suddenly, I was fully stimulated again and lusting for Jasmine's touch. I fantasized about her bending down and taking my swollen nub between her puffy lips and letting me come in her mouth.

Unfortunately, my satisfaction would have to wait a little longer. Instead, Jasmine reached into her bag and pulled out a straight-edge razor. In anyone else's hands, it might look threatening, especially in my prostrated and vulnerable position. But something about the way she delicately and sensuously opened the jackknifed tool instantly evaporated my fears. I could see how this type of razor would in fact give her better control safely cutting my stubs instead of the usual ladies plastic razor.

With her right hand, Jasmine gently laid the razor on its flat edge at the top of my mound, while she gently pulled my skin upwards with her other hand. Then she slowly turned the sharp edge perpendicular to my skin and began softly scraping the razor downwards. I could hear the bristling sound as the razor edge removed my nubs right down to the follicles. She repeated the pattern in one inch wide swipes on one side then the other of my pubis, being ever-so-careful to stop just where my clitoris lay quivering in a mixture of fear and excitement. There was something about the utter vulnerability of the procedure that made it the most erotic experience I'd ever had.

Jasmine used the same deft touch as she moved down my vulva and perineum, scraping the vestiges of stray hairs away with gentle swipes of the long blade, while sensuously separating my folds and flesh with her other hand. She took extra time and care around my anus and clit, using the gentlest and slowest motion I've ever felt someone apply to my body. The combination of fright and titillation as she probed my most sensitive body parts created a river of sensuous fluids running down my vulva. By this time, no shaving gel was necessary to provide a smooth gliding surface for the knife.

When she was finished, Jasmine retrieved a fresh wash towel from beside the sink and held it under the warm water faucet then twisted the excess water into the basin. She returned to the table and placed it over my splayed legs then gently cleansed the excess moisture and remaining shaving gel with gentle massaging movements of her hands. The warm, moist towel felt exquisite against my newly shaved skin. Jasmine's hands now felt comforting between my legs rather than erotic.

She had taken me on an incredibly sensuous erotic arc, right to the edge of ecstasy and back, to a quiet relaxed place. I exhaled fully and completely for the first time in almost an hour.

Jasmine removed the towel from between my legs and held up a large hand mirror at a forty-five degree angle toward me.

"What do you think?" she asked.

I tilted my head up and studied her masterpiece. Far from the usual red and swollen vulva that I typically experienced after the violent waxing with my regular esthetician, I'd never seen my pussy look so beautiful. Utterly bereft of any hair, my entire perineum from my pubic mound to my anus was totally bald, pink—and gorgeous. I just stared at my beautiful pussy, utterly transfixed by the transformation.

"You have to *feel* it to really appreciate how beautiful you are, Jade," Jasmine purred.

I moved my right hand down, running my fingers along the edges of my pussy. I gasped from a feeling I'd never felt before. It felt smooth as silk: no bumps or blemishes or cuts or bruises. It was almost as if I was feeling somebody else— somebody I'd never felt before. I couldn't stop my left hand joining the other in rubbing and caressing my sensitive organs.

Jasmine lowered the mirror and smiled at me as I felt the moisture begin to accumulate between my legs again.

"It's almost time for your dinner appointment," she said. "Why don't you save the best for last? I think you'll find plenty of ways to satisfy your appetite over the next couple of hours."

She lifted my kimono from the hook at the edge of the bathtub and held it open for me.

"I'll escort you downstairs now if you're ready. All you need to bring is your kimono and slippers—and your mask of course."

I sat up slowly and stepped off the massage table. Turning around, I held my arms out as Jasmine lifted one arm of the silk robe onto me then the other. Then she turned around to face me, wrapped the silk tie around me, and tied a single bow over my belly button. She retrieved my matching silk slippers and knelt down on one knee to gently lift my feet one at a time and place them softly inside. It took every ounce of my power not to grab her head and pull it into my pulsating pussy.

Jasmine stood up gracefully and smiled into my eyes.

"If you'll follow me, I'll escort you now to the fantasy feast."

She didn't bother putting her own robe on. Her tight little ass barely jiggled as she stepped smartly ahead of me. I wasn't sure if I'd have a chance to feel Jasmine's touch again before the evening was over, but for now I was in total bliss ogling her petite, curvaceous figure from behind...

Read More

# ABOUT THE AUTHOR

If you would like to receive notification of new book(s) in Jade's Erotic Adventures, follow me at http://bookbub.com/authors/victoria-rush.

If you have a moment, please post a brief review on my Amazon book page at viewbook.at/thedare . Even just a couple of sentences will help other readers find and enjoy this book as much as you hopefully did.

Follow, share, like, and comment at:

www.facebook.com/authorvictoriarush
www.pinterest.com/authorvictoriarush
www.twitter.com/authorvictoriarush
authorvictoriarush@outlook.com

Hope to see you again soon!